To the wild wolves of Yellowstone
and our own little wolf, Emmett John

Thanks to Kevan Atteberry for his technical assistance and
to photographer Max Waugh for his introduction to Yellowstone.
Text copyright © 2017 by Laura McGee Kvasnosky
Illustrations copyright © 2017 by Laura McGee Kvasnosky and Kate Harvey McGee

First edition 2017

Library of Congress Catalog Card Number pending
ISBN 978-0-7636-8971-1

17 18 19 20 21 22 CCP 10 9 8 7 6 5 4 3 2 1

Printed in Shenzhen, Guangdong, China

This book was typeset in Bembo.
The illustrations were done in gouache resist and colored digitally.

Candlewick Press
99 Dover Street
Somerville, Massachusetts 02144

visit us at www.candlewick.com

LITTLE WOLF'S
FIRST HOWLING

Laura McGee Kvasnosky
and Kate Harvey McGee

CANDLEWICK PRESS

LITTLE WOLF'S FATHER led the way straight to the top of the hill.
Little Wolf zigzagged behind, sniffing each outcrop and sage.
"Tonight's the night," said Big Wolf. "Your first howling."
Little Wolf's ears shivered with excitement. "I'm ready," he said.
"I am ready to howl!"

Father and son sat side by side. They watched as the stars blinked on and a full moon peeked over the mountain.

"Is it time yet?" said Little Wolf. "Can I howl now?"

"Hold on," said his father. "First, let me demonstrate proper howling form."

Big Wolf stood tall. He took a deep breath.
He lifted his muzzle to the sky and howled.

AAAAAAAA

AAOOOOOOOOOOOOOOOOOOOOOOOOOOOOOOOOOO

The last notes drifted out over the valley.
Little Wolf was thrilled to the tip of his tail.
"My turn now. Right, Dad? Here I go. Just like you."
Big Wolf nodded. "OK, Son. Give it a try."

Little Wolf stood tall. He took a deep breath.
He lifted his muzzle to the sky and howled.

aaaaaaaaaaaaaaaoooooooooo

Ooooooooooooooooooooooooooooooooooooo

I'm hoooowling, 'oooowling, 'ooooowling!

Big Wolf raised his eyebrows. "That was a good beginning," he said, "but your finish was not proper howling form. Let me demonstrate again."

AAAAAAAAAAAOOOOOO

"I got it. I got it," said Little Wolf.

Little Wolf lifted his muzzle to the sky and howled again.

aaaaaaaaaaaOO

Oooooooooooooooooooooooooooooooooooooooooo
dibbity dobbity skibbity skobbity
skooo-wooooo-wooooooooooo

Little Wolf looked over at his father. "What do you think, Dad?
Did you like it? Did you?"

Big Wolf sighed. "Son, I am proud of your nose, which has led to many new trails. I admire your strength when you tumble with the other pups. Most of all, I love how your ears express your thoughts. But your howling? It is not proper howling form."

Little Wolf hung his head.

"Let me demonstrate again," said Big Wolf.
"Listen closely."

AAAA

AAAAAOOOOOOOOOOOOOOOOOOOO

Each note rang clear and true and soared to the moon.
"Your turn," said Big Wolf.

Little Wolf's heart swelled with wildness and joy. He knew
it wasn't proper howling form, but he had to let loose.

skiddily skoddily beep bop, a bo
boppita boppita wheeee bop, a

oo booo boooooooooooooooooooooooooooooo

diddily daddily dooooooooooooooooooooooooooooo

Big Wolf listened closely.
His tail started wagging.
His ears started twitching.
His paws started tapping.
Big Wolf couldn't help it.

Big Wolf jumped in.

DIBBY, DIBBY DO-WOP A DOOOOOOOO!

Little Wolf grinned from ear to furry ear and howled back.

dibby, dibby do-wop a dooooooooo!

Skiddily skoddily beep bop a booo booo boo

BOPPITA BOPPITA WHEEEE BOP, A DID

dibbity dobbity skibbity

WE'RE HOOOWLING,

OOOO

DILY DADDILY DOOO

skobbity skooooo-wooo-wooooo

'OOWLING, 'OWLING TO THE MOOOOON!

Together they howled the moon to the top of the sky.

Little Wolf stuck close to his father as they trotted home.
"Wait until we tell the others," he said.
Big Wolf smiled. "Oh, I expect they already know."